not too small at all

a mouse tail tale

stephanie Z. Townsend

illustrated by Bill Looney

First Printing: January 2008
Third Printing: February 2017

Copyright © 2008 by Stephanie Z. Townsend. All rights reserved. No part of this book may be reproduced in any manner whatsoever without written permission of the publisher except in the case of brief quotations in articles and reviews.

Printed in China

For information write:
Master Books
P.O. Box 726
Green Forest, AR 72638

Please visit our website for other great titles:
www.masterbooks.com

ISBN 13: 978-0-89051-524-2
Library of Congress Number: 2007939084

not too small at all
a mouse ~~tail~~ tale

stephanie Z. Townsend
illustrated by Bill Looney

Dedicated to
Ben, London, and Clayton,
my little family of readers.

Grandpa pulled the colorful blanket right up under Benjamin and Daniel's chins and tucked it snuggly under the twig mattress. "Story time!" they sang out. Grandpa told the best stories! They were especially interesting because they were true stories about things the Creator God had done. Grandpa smiled, settled into his rocking chair, and began, "Once upon a time, long, long ago when I was a young mouse like you..."

He was interrupted by a tap at the little door. A large brown eye appeared, then disappeared, and a finger pushed a large piece of cookie into the room. "Goodnight," a voice whispered. "Sleep tight!" "Thank you Mrs. Noah!" Benjamin and Daniel cried. They loved visiting Grandma and Grandpa's house. Grandpa broke off a piece of cookie for each of them and they munched happily as he continued."

"When I was young, I lived alone in a small hole in a house in the city. I was very shy and I was afraid of everyone and everything — especially the dinosaurs! Even the smallest of them was much bigger than I was! But what bothered me the most was that all the other animals seemed to have some important job to do."

"The dogs helped their masters guard the sheep during the day and herd them into the fold each night. The oxen worked hard, muscles straining, pulling plows in the field so their masters could plant the seeds that would yield crops to feed the village. The birds flew busily from tree to tree gathering worms to feed their chirping families. Everyone had a very important job to do."

"One day, I decided that I was going to learn how to do all the things that the other animals did. The next morning I got up early and went out to the pasture with the dogs. They were friendly and said they would teach me to herd sheep. 'You just circle around them and if they start to leave the flock, you bark a little,' one explained. 'If they still don't listen, you may have to nip at their heels,' said another helpfully."

"I watched them for a while before I got up the courage to try it. I ran into a small straying group and was immediately surrounded by a mass of moving legs. I squeaked as ferociously as I could, but those sheep wouldn't listen to me! My squeak was much too soft, and when I tried to bite them, they just stepped on my head and my tail!"

"The next day I went out to the field with the oxen and asked them to teach me to plow. They just laughed and said, 'You're much too small! It takes a special animal to do this job.' I tried to follow them anyway, but I got stuck in the oozing mud and had to go home and take a bath."

"The next day I went into an orchard and found some birds looking for worms. 'You can't help us with this,' one said kindly, 'But we're building a nest for our new babies. Maybe you can find some soft grass for it.' I searched and searched the orchard floor for the softest, greenest pieces of grass. But when I tried to climb up to the nest I lost my balance, fell off the fence, and rolled down the hill. I was very discouraged. Maybe the oxen were right. I was too small to do anything important."

"The kind bird flew down to the grassy spot where I lay and landed softly beside me. 'Are you all right?' she asked. 'I think so.' I mumbled, testing my legs. 'We have been very busy,' she said, 'and I appreciate your help. But why do you want to build a nest?' 'Well,' I hesitated, but then my story came tumbling out. 'I'm too small.' I finished. 'I'll never be able to do anything useful.'"

"The bird thought for a second and then said, 'Yes, you are young and you are small, but God the Creator made you! And do you know why?' I shook my head. 'To glorify himself,' she said, her wings flapping excitedly. 'Look around you! See how all the things He made work together? Look at the sun and the moon and the stars. They glorify God by serving the purpose for which He created them. You are a mouse. You cannot be the sun and you cannot warm the earth with your rays. You cannot be the moon or the stars. It would be ridiculous to try! Neither can you be a dog or an ox or a bird! God made you a mouse and He loves you just the way you are!'

"The kind bird was right, and her words were comforting. God the Creator had made me a mouse for a reason. That night I went to bed and slept more peacefully than I had for a long time."

14

The next morning I woke as the sun came peeking up from behind the hills just like every other day, only this was no ordinary day. I could feel that something exciting was going to happen. I yawned and stretched and washed my face as usual, but I was alert and waiting. I began to eat my breakfast when suddenly I knew that God the Creator wanted me to go down into the valley where Noah and his sons were building an enormous wooden structure that they called an ark."

"From the time I was a very young mouse, I had avoided that valley whenever possible. There was so much activity and noise there! Men bustled about driving the oxen and dinosaurs that towed heavy loads of wood and pitch. And there were always groups of people there watching and laughing at Noah and his family. Noah often took time to try to explain to them that God had commanded him to build the ark to save them from the waters of a Flood that would destroy the whole world, but they just laughed even more."

"As I crept down into the valley, I noticed that many other animals were going in the same direction. As I walked toward the ark, I saw another mouse — a very beautiful mouse, I might add. And that's how I met your grandma." Benjamin and Daniel giggled into the covers.

"She said her name was Abigail and we ran down the hill together until we reached the open door of the ark. Because we were small, we were able to wriggle our way to the front. The air was filled with the sound of laughing and surprised chatter as townspeople gathered around the ark to watch young animals of all kinds walk calmly up the ramp two by two."

"For 40 days the rain fell. 'Praise God, this ark is our salvation' Noah kept saying. protected us from thunder, lightning, wind, and rain. Although we weren't sure what is going to happen to us, we knew that God the Creator had a purpose for us and would ep us safe no matter what happened. Often in the evenings Noah would talk to his mily about God's plan. He reminded them that God's heart had been grieved because the sin of the people of the earth, and that God had sent this worldwide flood as nishment for their wickedness. But God had provided a way of escape, a way to be ved from the waters of the flood."

"One day as I was walking through the ark, I heard a loud bawling coming from one of the cattle stalls. I scampered over and found that one of the young cows was twisted up and caught in her rope and couldn't get to her food and water. I looked around for Noah, but he was nowhere to be found, so I quickly squeezed through the stall door and started gnawing through the rope. It took me a long time, but finally the cow was free. 'Thank you!' she said. 'I was so thirsty and I didn't know if anyone could hear me. It's a good thing you were small enough to get through the gate!' I smiled. Being small — just the way God the Creator made me — had given me the opportunity to help someone else."

23

After 40 days, the rain stopped, but still the ark kept floating. One day, after we had been on the ark for nine long months, Noah released a raven and a dove into the sky. Only the little dove returned, because she couldn't find anywhere to rest. A week later Noah released the dove again and she came back with an olive branch in her mouth. 'That means plants and trees are growing,' Noah said. 'It won't be long now!' We were looking forward to getting back on solid ground! The next time Noah let the dove go we waited and waited, but she never came back and when it was time, God opened the ark's door."

"It was a brand new, fresh world reborn by water. Noah and his family fell to the ground thanking God and singing praises to Him, as they had so many times during our year on the ark. Noah built an altar and they offered a sacrifice to God. 'Look at the beautiful colors!' Mrs. Noah cried. God the Creator had put a rainbow in the sky as a promise that He would never again destroy the earth with water. I was glad that God's plan for me allowed me to be part of this brand new world."

"There was a lot of work to do. Noah and Mrs. Noah and their sons and their wives started building houses and the animals scattered to do the same. Your grandma and I loved Noah and Mrs. Noah so much that we decided to stay with them. Years passed, all the families of the earth grew and one day the two of you arrived! And I'm so glad that God's plan for me allowed me to be your grandpa!"

THE END

Not Too Small at All, A Mouse Tale author Stephanie Townsend hopes through reading this delightful story that children will understand how much God loves them and created each of them for a special purpose. A former special event coordinator at the Answers in Genesis ministry, she is a wife and a mother of two beautiful children (pictured with daughter London). A graduate of Bob Jones University and an avid traveler who appreciates experiencing new cultures and foods, *Not Too Small At All* is Stephanie's first book.

Bill Looney, to use the common vernacular, is a "natural" artist. Illustrating many Master Books including *The True Story of Noah's Ark.* A Christian since 1974, he desires to use his talents for the Lord. Bill attended the University of Texas at Arlington and Dallas Art Institute, and resides in the Dallas area.

THE VOYAGE BEGINS AGAIN

Williamstown, KY, South of Cincinnati

ENCOUNTER®